D0210853

HALFWAY TO PERFECT

A **DYAMONDE DANIEL** Book

Also by Nikki Grimes

Jazmin's Notebook

Bronx Masquerade

The Road to Paris

Make Way for Dyamonde Daniel

Rich: A Dyamonde Daniel Book

Almost Zero: A Dyamonde Daniel Book

HALFWAY TO PERFECT

A **DYAMONDE DANIEL** Book

Nikki Grimes

illustrated by
R. Gregory Christie

G. P. Putnam's Sons
An Imprint of Penguin Group (USA) Inc.

G. P. PUTNAM'S SONS

A division of Penguin Young Readers Group.

Published by The Penguin Group.

Penguin Group (USA) Inc., 375 Hudson Street, New York, NY 10014, U.S.A.

Penguin Group (Canada), 90 Eglinton Avenue East, Suite 700, Toronto,

Ontario M4P 2Y3, Canada (a division of Pearson Penguin Canada Inc.).

Penguin Books Ltd, 80 Strand, London WC2R 0RL, England.

Penguin Ireland, 25 St. Stephen's Green, Dublin 2, Ireland

(a division of Penguin Books Ltd).

Penguin Group (Australia), 250 Camberwell Road, Camberwell, Victoria 3124,

Australia (a division of Pearson Australia Group Pty Ltd).

Penguin Books India Pvt Ltd, 11 Community Centre, Panchsheel Park,

New Delhi—110 017, India.

Penguin Group (NZ), 67 Apollo Drive, Rosedale, Auckland 0632, New Zealand

(a division of Pearson New Zealand Ltd).

Penguin Books (South Africa) (Pty) Ltd, 24 Sturdee Avenue, Rosebank,

Johannesburg 2196, South Africa.

Penguin Books Ltd, Registered Offices: 80 Strand, London WC2R 0RL, England.

Printed in the United States of America. Text set in Bembo Semibold.

Library of Congress Cataloging-in-Publication Data
Grimes, Nikki. Halfway to perfect : a Dyamonde Daniel book / Nikki Grimes ;
illustrated by R. Gregory Christie. p. cm. Summary: Despite what Dyamonde and
Free say, Damaris worries that she is getting fat, until a classmate's problem with
diabetes causes her to change her thoughts about body image.
[1. Body image—Fiction. 2. Diabetes—Fiction. 3. Schools—Fiction. 4. African
Americans—Fiction.] I. Christie, R. Gregory, 1971– ill. II. Title.
PZ7.G88429Hal 2012 [E]—dc23 2011045960
ISBN 978-0-399-25178-8
3 5 7 9 10 8 6 4

Contents

"Young readers will wish
they had a friend like Dyamonde."
—*Kirkus Reviews*

The World of Dyamonde Daniel

Dyamonde

This third-grader loves food, especially her mom's home cooking! Dyamonde is super smart, but even she doesn't have all the answers—and she wonders why looks are so important to some people.

Free

Dyamonde's best friend has a bottomless stomach—this boy sure can eat. He can't imagine going on a diet. He always has room for more!

Damaris

She has a million amazing qualities, but lately she's been feeling less than sure of herself—so it might be time for Dyamonde to remind her that she's perfect just the way she is.

Amberline

Amberline acts like she doesn't want any friends. She doesn't seem to care what anyone thinks of her, but could there be more to her story than her classmates realize?

The Three T's

Tanya, Tylisha and Tameeka talk about the most ridiculous things, like how important it is to look and act a certain way. They haven't yet learned that it's what's inside that counts.

Dyamonde's mom

Nothing beats her spaghetti and meatballs, except maybe her Saturday morning pancakes. But sometimes she has to remind her super-smart daughter that veggies are great, too!

Spaghetti Heaven

You'd never know it to look at her skinny little self, but Dyamonde loves food. If there were a class in eating, she'd get an A plus every time.

Dyamonde treats all food fairly. She likes Mexican tacos, Chinese egg rolls, and Cuban beans and rice. She eats beef hot dogs, turkey burgers and fried chicken. Actually, she likes just about anything that has chicken in it: noodle soup, pot-pie, even chicken salad sandwiches.

Dyamonde doesn't have much use for vegetables, but she loves broccoli, mostly because each spear looks like a tree. And she loves fruit—especially peaches, cherries, and grapes of any size or color. Dyamonde also loves some foods that other people don't, like cottage cheese and applesauce mixed together.

"Yuck!" said Free the first time he saw her eat some.

"Oh, *puleeze!*" said Dyamonde, stirring in a little more applesauce. "You just wish you had a bowlful!"

Yes, Dyamonde loves all sorts of food, but her absolute favorite food in the whole wide world is spaghetti and meatballs with garlic bread. And guess what Mrs. Daniel had made the last time Free and Damaris came over?

Dyamonde couldn't wait to sit down for dinner. The minute the bowl of spaghetti was placed on the table, Dyamonde's mouth began to water. Free licked his lips and reached for the bowl.

Dyamonde cut her eyes at Free with a look that said, *Not yet!* Damaris closed her eyes and waited until Mrs. Daniel finished saying grace, then she reached for the basket of garlic bread.

"Don't forget the salad," said Mrs. Daniel. Dyamonde scrunched up her nose, but she grabbed a few lettuce leaves to make her mom happy. Free plucked out a couple of tomatoes and a slice of cucumber, but Damaris filled up her whole salad plate.

"Yum," said Damaris.

"Double yum!" said Free, his

mouth already smeared with spaghetti sauce.

"Gross!" said Dyamonde. But Free ignored her. He was too busy making his tummy happy.

Mrs. Daniel smiled, especially when Damaris asked for seconds.

Free looked like one of those cartoon chipmunks, his cheeks were so full of food. Mrs. Daniel shook her head.

"Free, if you don't watch it," she said, "you'll blow up like a balloon!"

"Yeah," said Dyamonde. "Then I'll have to poke a hole in you and watch you fly around the room backwards till all the air comes out!"

Dyamonde and Free looked at each other and laughed.

Damaris didn't laugh, though. She just put down her fork, saying she was full.

"What about dessert?" asked Mrs. Daniel. "You saved room for that, didn't you?"

"No, thank you," whispered Damaris. "I think I've had enough."

Free shrugged. "More for me!" he said, grinning. But something

in Damaris's voice bothered Dyamonde.

"Are you okay?" she asked her
friend.

Damaris nodded, so Dyamonde
let it drop.

The Girl in the Mirror

Dyamonde was amazed at the silly things kids talked about at school. Take the next day. Dyamonde was in the girls' room, taking care of her business, when she overheard three girls blabbing away over the loud sputter of the water faucet going full blast. It was the Three T's, Tanya, Tylisha and Tameeka. Dyamonde would know their voices anywhere. Damaris was there too, but Dyamonde didn't know it.

"Well, I may be the youngest in class," said Tylisha, "but I also weigh the least."

"So what?" said Tanya. "I'm the most popular."

"You wish!" said Tylisha.

"Ugh!" said Tanya. "I've got to go on a diet. I don't want to turn into a little piggy like Amberline."

"She's not *that* big," said Tameeka.

"Are you kidding? Have you seen her pouchy belly?" asked Tylisha.

"Oh," said Tameeka. "Yeah."

"She must be stuffing her face when no one's watching," said Tanya.

"Like when she's by herself," said Tameeka.

"Which is all the time, since nobody wants to be her friend," said Tylisha.

"I know!" said Tameeka. "It's sad."

"Well, it's her own fault," said Tylisha. "That's what she gets for being so pushy."

After that, Dyamonde heard the faucet switch off. The girls' voices faded away as the three left, their sneakers squeaking against the tile floor.

Dyamonde straightened her clothes and went to wash her hands. That's when she saw Damaris pinching her waist and frowning at her reflection in the mirror.

"What's the matter?" asked Dyamonde.

Damaris dropped her arms to her sides when she realized Dyamonde was there staring at her.

"You scared me!" said Damaris.

"Sorry," said Dyamonde. "But what's wrong?"

"Nothing," said Damaris, switching on the faucet.

"Then how come your face is all scrunched up like you're about ready to cry?"

Damaris bit her lip, scrubbing her hands as if they had never been washed.

"It's no big deal," she said.

Dyamonde wasn't having it. She knew something was wrong. She crossed her arms and waited, staring Damaris down.

After a minute of this, Damaris

felt her shoulders sag. She dried her hands and turned to face her friend.

"I think I'm getting fat," said Damaris, almost in a whisper.

Dyamonde blinked. "What?"

"I think I'm getting fat."

Dyamonde started to laugh, but Damaris gave her such a sharp look, Dyamonde stopped mid-giggle.

"I'm sorry," said Dyamonde, "but who told you that?"

"Nobody. But you heard them call Amberline a piggy, right?"

Dyamonde nodded.

"Well, I'm practically the same size as Amberline, so I must look like a piggy too."

"No, you don't!" said Dyamonde. "They were just being mean. Amberline is not fat, and neither are you."

Damaris did not look convinced.

Dyamonde put her hands on Damaris's shoulders and spun her around to face the mirror again.

"Look at you," said Dyamonde. "You are perfect just the way you are."

Dyamonde gave Damaris a squeeze.

"Maybe not as perfect as *me*," said Dyamonde, "but you're at least halfway, and that's pretty close!"

Damaris was surprised to see her lips curling into a little smile.

Dyamonde bumped hips with her. "Let's get out of here," she said.

Damaris followed Dyamonde out into the hall. Dyamonde didn't know it, but by the time the girls reached homeroom, Damaris's smile had slipped away.

Crazy for Carrots

"Ooooh!" said Dyamonde later that day when she and her friends entered the lunchroom. "Check out the menu. They've got chicken nuggets and mashed potatoes. Yum!" Dyamonde licked her lips. Her taste buds began to sing before she'd even taken the first bite.

"Now *this* is what I'm talking about!" said Free, digging in. "This is way better than that nasty meat loaf they had yesterday." Those were the last words Free spoke until his plate was clean. He was too busy shoveling food into his mouth to talk.

"Dang, Free!" said Dyamonde. "You act like you've never seen food before in your life!" Free grunted and stuffed another forkful of food into his mouth.

Hopeless, thought Dyamonde.

Just then, Tylisha passed by, took one look at the plate in front of

Damaris and whispered in her ear, "If I had your hips, I'd skip the mashed potatoes." Then she joined Tanya and Tameeka at another table.

Damaris winced.

"What?" asked Dyamonde. "What did she say?"

Damaris made herself shrug. "Nothing," she said.

Dyamonde didn't believe her, but she didn't press.

Damaris glanced around the cafeteria and noticed Amberline sitting nearby, nibbling on a carrot. Damaris immediately sucked in her stomach and sat up a little straighter. Then she picked up a baby carrot with her fork and took a teensy bite.

"Summer break is almost here," said Damaris.

"Three weeks!" said Dyamonde.

"You know what that means," said Damaris.

"Picnics," said Dyamonde.

"Trips to the zoo," said Damaris.

"Italian ices!" said Dyamonde.

"The city swimming pool!" said Damaris.

"Cotton candy," said Dyamonde.

Both girls put their forks down.

"Coney Island!" they said in one voice.

Free burped loud enough to remind them that he was there.

"You did *not* just do that!" said Dyamonde.

"What?" asked Free, all innocent.

"Oh, *puleeze!*" said Dyamonde. She shook her head. *That boy has no manners!*

Dyamonde turned her attention back to her meal, stabbing her fork into one chicken nugget after another until they were all gone. She was scraping the last bit of potato off her plate when she noticed that Damaris's plate was still full.

"Why aren't you eating?" asked Dyamonde.

"What are you talking about?" asked Damaris. "Didn't you just see me make those carrots disappear?"

"Yeah, but you hardly touched anything else," said Dyamonde.

"Well," said Damaris, "I guess I'm just not that hungry."

"Okay," said Dyamonde, not sure whether to believe her friend.

"Hey, if you're not eating those nuggets, can I have 'em?" asked Free.

Damaris nodded, pushing her plate across the table. She finished off her carrots and then the three friends headed out to the school yard until the bell rang.

Dyamonde stole a few glances at Damaris, wondering if her friend had told the truth about not being hungry. Dyamonde got her answer back in the classroom when she heard her friend's stomach growl.

For the next couple of days, Dyamonde studied Damaris at lunchtime to see how much she ate, and every day she watched Damaris move food around her plate without actually eating more than a bite or two. Dyamonde started to worry about her friend, especially when she noticed Damaris's blue jeans starting to sag.

"I know what you're doing," Dyamonde whispered to her one afternoon. "You're dieting, aren't you?" It was more of an accusation than a question.

Damaris shrugged. "So what?"

"I knew it!" said Dyamonde. "But why?"

"You wouldn't understand," said Damaris. "You're already like a toothpick, but I need to lose weight."

"No," said Dyamonde, "you don't. I already told you that you are fine just the way you are."

Damaris shook her head. "You're just saying that because you're my friend."

"No, I'm not," said Dyamonde. "I mean, yeah, I'm your friend. But that's not why I said it."

"Look, I don't want to talk about this anymore, okay?" begged Damaris.

"Okay," said Dyamonde. But

it wasn't. Dyamonde was worried about her friend. She'd seen pictures of girls who practically looked like skeletons from dieting too much. She didn't want to see that happen to Damaris.

I wish I could make Damaris see herself like I do, thought Dyamonde. *But how?*

Coney Island Surprise

"Your birthday is coming up next weekend," said Mrs. Daniel over dinner, as if Dyamonde weren't counting down the days. "I was wondering if you'd thought about what you'd like to do on Saturday to celebrate, where you'd like to—"

"Coney Island!" said Dyamonde.

"Well," said Mrs. Daniel, "that was easy."

"And can I bring Free and Damaris? Please, please, please?"

Mrs. Daniel smiled. "I'll give their parents a call."

Dyamonde bounced up and down on her chair, too excited to speak.

At ten o'clock Saturday morning, the foursome set foot on the Coney Island boardwalk. The minute they were there, Dyamonde remembered the Coney Island fun-house mirrors.

That's it! thought Dyamonde. *If Damaris looks at herself in all those different mirrors, maybe she'll understand that there are different ways of seeing herself and they're not all real. Anyway, it's worth a try. I'll take her by the mirrors later.*

The first thing Dyamonde did was to make a dash for the carousel. Free called it a baby ride, but Dyamonde didn't care. She loved it, and so did Damaris. The Ferris wheel came next, then the roller coaster. Free and Dyamonde braved that alone, leaving Damaris and Mrs. Daniel waving to them from the ground. All that riding in circles and screaming their lungs out on the roller coaster made everyone hungry. Dyamonde's mom told her she could have whatever she wanted.

"It is your birthday," said Mrs. Daniel.

They all bought Nathan's hot dogs and washed them down with cola. Free ate ice cream for dessert, but Dyamonde chose cotton candy. Damaris skipped dessert altogether, choosing to sip some lemonade instead.

"I can have ice cream any old

time," said Dyamonde. "But cotton candy is special—like my birthday."

Dyamonde enjoyed every mouthful of her sticky treat, especially the way it melted on her tongue.

"Yum!" said Dyamonde. "You don't know what you're missing."

"Oh yeah? Well, my ice cream is chocolaty, super yummy, mm-mm good," said Free.

"Not as scrumptious as my melty pink cloud of deliciousness," said Dyamonde. She tore off a big piece of it and hummed as it disappeared on her tongue.

"Whatever," said Free. "I bet I'll finish mine first."

"Suit yourself," said Dyamonde. "I don't get cotton candy every day, so I'm taking my sweet time."

"Hey! That's good. Cotton candy, sweet time. Very punny!"

"Don't you mean *funny*?" said Dyamonde. "As in, you think you're so funny?"

"Ha, ha, ha," said Free between licks. "Just forget it."

Damaris laughed at them both, then sipped the last of her lemonade.

When they were done eating, Free's attention turned to the beach.

"Last one in the water is a rotten egg!" said Free.

As if on cue, Dyamonde, Damaris and Free started race walking to the steps that led down to the beach.

At the bottom of the stairs, they shimmied out of the clothes covering their bathing suits and slipped off their sandals. The second their toes hit the sand, they took off, dodging beach umbrellas and picnic blankets, running toward the waves as they broke on the shore.

Damaris splashed around for a few minutes, then climbed out of the water.

"Hey!" said Dyamonde, splashing around in the cool water. "I can't believe you're leaving already!"

"I've had enough for now," said Damaris.

"Oh, man!" said Free. "I could stay in here forever."

"Me too," said Dyamonde. She watched Damaris bend down to pick up shells.

She's getting way too thin, thought Dyamonde. *I have to say something, but not with Free around. Maybe this would be a good time to find those fun-house mirrors.*

Dyamonde waded over to Damaris. "My skin is getting all wrinkly," she said. "I want to go back up on the boardwalk for a while. Want to come?"

"Okay," said Damaris.

"Hey!" said Free when he saw the girls leaving the beach. "Where're you going?"

"It's girls' stuff!" Dyamonde yelled. "We won't be gone long."

Free shrugged and dove back into the waves. Mrs. Daniel stayed behind to watch him.

Strolling on the boardwalk, Dyamonde took Damaris right to the Coney Island Museum. When Dyamonde saw all the fun-house mirrors, she squealed.

"Look at me! Look at me!" she said, posing and making faces in front of one of the mirrors. Damaris looked at her friend's reflection in the mirror and laughed. Dyamonde looked ten feet tall, and thin as paper.

"*Now* look at me!" said

Dyamonde, jumping in front of the second mirror. This time, Dyamonde looked short and fat, like one of the round Munchkins in *The Wizard of Oz.*

Damaris laughed at that reflection too.

"Now it's your turn," said Dyamonde, nudging her friend to stand in front of the first mirror. "Is that the real Damaris?"

"No!" said Damaris, giggling.

Next, Dyamonde led her friend to stand in front of the second mirror. "Is this the real Damaris?" asked Dyamonde.

"No, silly!" said Damaris.

Then Dyamonde locked arms with Damaris and walked her over to the third mirror, which was regular.

"That's the real Damaris," said Dyamonde in a soft voice. "Not super tall and super skinny. Not extra short and fat. The *real* Damaris is somewhere in the middle, and all you have to do to see her is to look in the right mirror."

Dyamonde was quiet for a moment, letting her words sink in.

"Those kids at school," said Dyamonde. "You can't listen to

them, Damaris. They're all looking in the wrong mirror. Okay?"

Damaris gave her friend an embarrassed smile.

Damaris nodded in silence. Then she gave Dyamonde a tight squeeze.

This Little Piggy

It took about a week for Free to notice that Damaris had gone back to eating like normal.

"I thought you were on a diet," said Free one day at lunch.

"Not anymore," said Damaris after washing down a spoonful of macaroni and cheese with a swig of chocolate milk. "I'm done with all that."

"That's too bad," said Free. "I was kind of getting used to eating your fries."

"Free!" said Dyamonde.

"What?" Free gave Dyamonde his innocent look. "I'm a growing boy."

"Oh. So that's why your head's so fat," said Dyamonde. Free stuck his tongue out at her and turned his attention back to Damaris.

"I don't know why you were dieting in the first place," he said. "It's not like you needed to."

Dyamonde and Damaris shared a secret smile.

Dyamonde wasn't done keeping an eye on Damaris, though. Every now and then, she still caught Damaris staring long and hard at herself in the mirror. What's more, whenever one of the super-skinny girls from class passed by, Damaris watched them with envy. And there was one more thing. Damaris started watching Amberline.

Take yesterday. Dyamonde and Damaris were standing in the lunch line, minding their own business, reading the menu.

"I can't make up my mind," said Dyamonde. "Should I have pepperoni pizza? I love pizza, but I can't stand pepperoni."

"You could just pick them off and give them to Free," said Damaris.

"True," said Dyamonde. "That boy will eat anything!"

"Make up your mind already!" came a sharp voice from behind them. Dyamonde and Damaris spun around and saw Amberline. Damaris instantly sucked in her stomach.

"What's the big hurry?" asked

Dyamonde, who didn't like being yelled at. "Just give me a sec."

But Amberline just pushed past the girls and cut in front of them. "Oh, forget this. I'm not waiting," she said.

The nerve! thought Dyamonde.

"Uh-oh," said Tanya, who was at the front of the line. "Here comes Miss Piggy." Damaris winced, waiting for Amberline to react. But Amberline acted as if she hadn't even heard the insult.

Dyamonde shook her head and went back to studying the menu.

"Okay. Pizza it is," Dyamonde

decided. From the corner of her eye, she noticed Damaris staring after Amberline with a look of awe on her face.

"Did you see that?" asked Damaris.

"What, Amberline being *rude*? Yeah, who could miss it?"

"No, not that," said Damaris. "They called her Miss Piggy and she didn't even blink."

"So?" asked Dyamonde.

"So, I wish I could do that," said Damaris. "She doesn't seem to care what other people say about her. Not like me."

"Yeah, well," said Dyamonde. "That girl is nobody to be jealous of."

Damaris stiffened. "Who said I was jealous?" she asked.

"Oh, *puleeze*," said Dyamonde.

"I'm not jealous. I'm not! It's just . . . if somebody called me fat, it would really bother me. But Amberline doesn't care what other people think," said Damaris. "I wish I could be like that."

"Well, they better not call you fat when I'm around," said Dyamonde.

Damaris smiled at that.

"Even if they do, I'm not going

to start dieting again," said Damaris, "so don't worry."

But Dyamonde was worried.

"Look, Damaris, I—"

"Hey!" said Free, joining them in line. "What're you two yammering about?"

"Nothing," said Damaris.

"Nothing," echoed Dyamonde. But Dyamonde's nothing was like a heavy stone in her pocket, weighing her down for the rest of the day.

Feeling Faint

Dyamonde studied Damaris day after day, watching to see if she would skip the french fries or the chicken nuggets or the pizza when those foods turned up on the lunch menu. But Damaris never did.

I'm still worried, thought Dyamonde, eyeing her friend in class. *She's still not comfortable with herself.*

Dyamonde knew she was right. She'd noticed that Damaris had stopped wearing belts and always seemed to be trying to stretch out her shirts so they would come farther down over her hips. *She may not be on a diet,* thought Dyamonde, *but she's still not happy.* Dyamonde wasn't sure what to say or do about it, though.

"Well, Dyamonde?" said Mrs. Cordell. "Can you tell me the answer?"

Dyamonde looked up at her teacher, blinking.

"I'm sorry?" said Dyamonde.

"You should be," said Mrs. Cordell. "Try to pay atten—"

Just then, the bell went off, signaling a fire drill.

"All right, class," said Mrs. Cordell. "Line up. Quickly!"

In all the rush and shuffle, Damaris and Amberline ended up side by side. Right away, Damaris sucked in her stomach and stood a little straighter. Damaris didn't want anybody calling *her* Miss Piggy just because she was next to Amberline.

Damaris wanted to talk to Amberline, to ask her if she really didn't care when kids called her fat or if she was just pretending. Damaris wanted to ask Amberline lots of things, but Amberline kept her mouth shut tight and looked straight ahead as if Damaris wasn't even there.

Why is Amberline like that? Damaris wasn't sure if she'd ever know.

The class marched outside and stood for a few minutes, fidgeting, until the bell rang for them to go back to their classrooms.

On the way in, Dyamonde heard a scream.

"That's Damaris!" whispered

Dyamonde, following the voice. She saw her friend kneeling on the sidewalk, bent over someone lying still on the ground. As Dyamonde got closer, she saw that the someone was Amberline.

"Get the nurse!" ordered Damaris. "Hurry!"

D Is for Diabetes

"Coming through! Coming through!" called Ms. Matsuda, the school nurse.

"Annette!" said Mrs. Cordell. "Thank God you're here."

Ms. Matsuda nodded to Mrs. Cordell, then pushed past the gawking students to reach Amberline. Damaris moved aside but stayed within hearing range. Dyamonde and Free were right behind her.

"Students, stand back," ordered Ms. Matsuda. She knelt on the ground beside Amberline and rolled the girl on her side, just in case she became nauseated. Then she pricked one of Amberline's fingers, put a plastic strip on her drop of blood and inserted it into a small machine. She read the number that appeared on the screen, then quickly wiped a spot on Amberline's upper right arm with an alcohol swab and injected her with some medicine.

In no time, it seemed, the girl's eyes fluttered open.

"What happened?" whispered Amberline, surprised to find half the class staring down at her.

"You fainted," said Damaris.

Amberline tried to sit up.

"Easy," said Ms. Matsuda, helping her. "I'm guessing you skipped breakfast this morning." It was not a question.

Amberline nodded, looking embarrassed.

"I woke up late, and I didn't want to miss the bell," said Amberline.

"You know you can't skip

meals," said Ms. Matsuda in a low voice.

"I know," muttered Amberline. "My mom always tells me, 'Diabetes is nothing to fool around with.'"

Diabetes! The word made Damaris shiver.

"Diabetes," whispered Dyamonde. She had heard the word too.

"Man," whispered Free. "That's some serious stuff."

Ms. Matsuda looked around nervously. This information was supposed to be private. If Amberline had fainted in the classroom, all the students would have been sent out into the hall while the nurse treated Amberline. But this happened outside on the street, and there was nowhere to send the class.

"Okay, class." Mrs. Cordell clapped her hands to get everyone's attention. "The show is over. Head back to homeroom and take your seats."

"But what about Amberline?" asked Damaris.

Mrs. Cordell gave her shoulder a squeeze. "Don't worry about

Amberline," she said. "Ms. Matsuda will take good care of her. Come on. Let's go."

Reluctantly, Damaris joined the rest of the class and filed back into the school.

Beehive

Wow, thought Dyamonde, stepping into the classroom. *I'll bet this is what a beehive sounds like.*

Everybody in the room was buzzing.

"Man! Did you see that?"

"What's wrong with Amberline?"

"She's got diabetes."

"What's that?"

"I thought that was an old folks' disease."

"Don't you have to be super fat to get that?"

"Yeah. That's what I thought."

"Amberline isn't even chubby."

"My grandma has that, and she's older than dirt."

"My uncle too. Plus he's all roly-poly."

"All right!" said Mrs. Cordell. "That's enough! Please take your seats."

The buzzing died down, but only a little.

Everyone was full of questions, including Dyamonde.

How come kids can get diabetes? What if I have it? How would I know? I sure don't want to fall over in the street one day, like Amberline.

The very thought of the possibility made Dyamonde's heart beat faster.

"Okay, class," said Mrs. Cordell. "Simmer down."

Dyamonde took a deep breath. Everyone else did too.

"Obviously, you all have questions about what just happened," said Mrs. Cordell, "so let's talk about it."

Finally, the class got quiet.

"For those of you who haven't already heard, Amberline has a condition called diabetes. Diabetes has something to do with the sugar inside your body.

"When your body is healthy, it breaks down the sugar and sends it out to all the cells so that they can use it for energy. But when you have diabetes, your body can't break down the sugar. Instead, all the sugar stays in the plasma stream and doesn't get into the cells, and that causes all kinds of problems throughout the body. Does that make sense?" asked Mrs. Cordell.

"Sort of," said Dyamonde, speaking for everyone.

"But what does that have to do with fainting?" asked Damaris.

"Yeah," said another student.

Mrs. Cordell pursed her lips, thinking.

"Fainting is one of the things that happens when you have too much or too little sugar in your blood. That's why a person with diabetes has to be careful about what they eat, and they can't skip meals."

Dyamonde and Damaris traded glances.

That's what the nurse said, thought Damaris. *Amberline skipped breakfast.*

"They also have to remember to take their insulin."

Several hands shot up around the room. It seemed everybody had more questions.

"That's it for now," announced Mrs. Cordell.

Free groaned, and he wasn't the only one.

"I need you to open your readers. If you have any more questions about diabetes, see me after school. Okay? Readers open."

Dyamonde wanted to know more, and so did Damaris. They looked at each other and mouthed the word *library.*

After school that day, they waved good-bye to Free, who jogged home alone.

"Let me know what you find," he said before taking off. "I have to get home and help my gram with the laundry. My mom said she was going to call and check."

The girls headed for the public library. As soon as they got there, they went straight to the information desk.

"We need to read about diabetes," said Dyamonde.

"It's important," said Damaris. "Can you help us?"

The librarian gave them a serious nod. "Yes, I can. But there are different types of diabetes, so it would help if I knew what made you interested."

Dyamonde nodded to her friend.

"Okay," said Damaris. "Well, it all started this morning . . ."

A Heavy Heart

The next day, Amberline came back to school.

Dyamonde noticed that she wasn't walking as tall and straight as she usually did. In fact, Amberline sort of shuffled into the room, staring down at the floor. When she reached her seat, she slumped down into it, her eyes still on the floor.

I'll bet she's embarrassed, thought Dyamonde. *I would be.*

Mrs. Cordell began taking attendance. When she got to Amberline's name, she stopped and looked up from the attendance sheet.

"Welcome back, Amberline," said Mrs. Cordell. The minute she said it, all eyes turned on Amberline, who slid down in her seat even farther. Mrs. Cordell immediately realized her mistake.

"Eyes front," she ordered. Then she rushed on to the next names on the roll.

"Malik Simmons."

"Here."

"Gerald Thompson."

"Here!"

The entire time Mrs. Cordell took attendance, Damaris stared in Amberline's direction. Amberline must have felt her staring, but she never looked back at Damaris.

After lunch, Damaris went looking for Amberline in the school yard and Dyamonde tagged along.

They found the girl sitting on a bench, kicking the pebbles beneath her feet.

"Hello," said Damaris.

"Hey," said Dyamonde.

"Hey," said Amberline without looking up. Damaris waited and waited for Amberline to say something else.

Dyamonde couldn't stand the silence. "I'm glad you're okay," she said.

"Yeah," said Damaris. "That was pretty scary yesterday."

Amberline shrugged. "I'm fine now," she said.

"Good," said Damaris. Again, Damaris waited for Amberline to say more. She didn't.

Okay, thought Dyamonde. *Let's get out of here.*

She poked Damaris to give her a hint. Instead of turning to leave, Damaris cleared her throat and sat down.

"I was reading about diabetes last night," said Damaris. Amberline stopped kicking the dirt and raised her head. Damaris went on. "The book said when you have diabetes, you have to watch what you eat."

"I know," whispered Amberline.

"Actually, Mrs. Cordell said that too. And the book said you can't eat too many sweets," said Damaris.

"I know," said Amberline, a little louder.

"And it's really not a good thing to skip meals," Damaris continued.

"I know!" snapped Amberline.

Damaris flinched as if someone had slapped her in the face.

Amberline jumped up from the bench. "I know all that stuff already! You think I don't? I've known it half my life!" she yelled.

Damaris was red in the face

now. Still, she shot right back, "But you fainted, Amberline! And all because you didn't eat breakfast! Why would you do that if you knew?"

"You don't understand," said Amberline. "I get tired, Damaris. I get tired of always having to think about what I can eat and drink, and what I can't. I get tired of testing my blood sugar four times a day, and trying to remember to drink enough water, and making sure I eat on time. I get tired of all of it! You know what I wish?" asked Amberline. "I wish I could be a normal kid—so sometimes I act like one. That's all."

Amberline seemed to run out of words and out of air. She fell back onto the bench and sighed heavily.

In the silence, Damaris whispered, "I'm sorry."

Amberline turned to Damaris and stared deep into her eyes for a moment. "You have no idea how lucky you are," she said. "No idea. Now, just leave me alone." There were tears in Amberline's eyes.

Dyamonde stood up first and pulled Damaris after her. Damaris shuffled along, her feet as heavy as her heart. Dyamonde felt bad for her friend.

I wish I knew what to say, thought Dyamonde. But she didn't, so she just put her arm around Damaris's shoulders and walked her back to class.

Better than Normal

It took a few days, but the kids at school eventually stopped talking about Amberline and her diabetes.

Now it all made sense. Amberline stayed to herself so she could take her insulin in secret and not let anyone find out. And she didn't care about kids calling her fat because she had more serious things to worry about than some dumb kid's insult. And she probably acted mean on purpose, just to keep people far away. It all made sense to Dyamonde and Damaris now.

But Dyamonde and Damaris decided they weren't going to let Amberline push them away anymore. They were going to try to make friends with her.

Everybody needs friends, thought Dyamonde.

Damaris kept an eye out for Amberline at lunchtime.

"Hey, Amberline!" called Damaris one day. "Come sit with us."

"Yeah," said Dyamonde. "There's plenty of room at our table."

Amberline looked at Dyamonde and Damaris as if they each had two heads.

"What? Are we friends all of a sudden? I don't think so," said Amberline. Then she walked away before they could say anything more.

Dyamonde shrugged. "I guess the old Amberline is back," she said.

"I guess," said Damaris. "She must be so lonely, though. I feel sorry for her."

"Me too," said Dyamonde. "But you can't make somebody be your friend. They get to choose."

Damaris sighed. "You're right."

"I'm glad you chose to be my friend," said Dyamonde.

Those words made Damaris break into a smile. She turned to her friend and gave her a big hug.

"What's all this huggy-huggy stuff?" asked Free as he reached the table. He plopped his tray down across from them. "I hope you're not planning on hugging me!" He made a face.

"Oh, puleeze!" said Dyamonde. "You wish somebody would give you a hug."

"Not even!" said Free. "That's girly stuff. I look girly to you? No, so forget it. Hey, Damaris, you got too many fries on your plate. Can I have some?"

Damaris smacked his hand. "Get your fingers off my property!" she said.

The three friends laughed, then made all the food on their plates disappear.

In the days that followed, Damaris went back to being her old self. She gave up staring at herself in the mirror, Dyamonde noticed. And she stopped paying attention to anyone's dumb comments and wishing she was skinny all the time.

This suited Dyamonde just fine, because she was eager to have Damaris come to her house for a sleepover, and sleepovers at Dyamonde's house meant waking up to homemade banana pancakes covered in buttery maple syrup. Nobody ever got skinny eating those!

"Damaris," said Dyamonde one day, "ask your mom if you can come spend the night on Friday."

"Will your mom be making pancakes?" asked Damaris.

"Yup," said Dyamonde.

"Yum!" said Damaris. "I'll ask my mom tonight."

"Pancakes?" said Free. He licked his lips. "Can I come?"

"Puleeze!" said Dyamonde. "This is for girls only!"

Free groaned loud enough for the whole school to hear him.

That Saturday, Dyamonde and Damaris rushed to the breakfast

table and munched through a stack of pancakes in record time. Both girls went back for seconds.

Damaris had lifted the bottle of maple syrup, ready to pour some on her plate, when she stopped in midair. She put the bottle back on the table and sighed.

"What's the matter?" asked Dyamonde.

Damaris was lost in thought. It took her a minute to snap out of it.

"Damaris?"

"Huh? Oh. Sorry," she said. "I was just thinking Amberline was right."

Dyamonde licked syrup from the corner of her mouth before it could drip onto her pajamas. "Right about what?" she asked.

"About me being lucky. Here I was all worried about being called Miss Piggy like Amberline or not being skinny enough, and I never thought about how lucky I was to be healthy."

Dyamonde nodded.

"I don't have diabetes, so I can eat whatever I want and I don't have to think about it."

"Well," said Mrs. Daniel, interrupting, "that's not entirely true. If you want to stay healthy, you still need to make sure you eat your vegetables, drink enough milk and water, and get plenty of rest and exercise."

"I guess," said Damaris. "Still."

"Still," added Dyamonde, "we don't have to prick our fingers to check our blood every day, or get shots, or think about how much sugar is in everything we eat."

"Yeah," said Damaris. "That must be hard."

"Well," said Mrs. Daniel, "since you know that, I hope you're both being extra nice to that girl."

"We tried," whispered Damaris.

"We can try again," Dyamonde whispered back. Damaris nodded.

"What's the girl's name?" asked Mrs. Daniel.

"Amberline," Dyamonde and Damaris said in unison.

"Amberline! Now that's a mouthful!" said Mrs. Daniel. Dyamonde and Damaris smiled. "Now quit hogging that syrup and hand it over," Mrs. Daniel said to Damaris.

"Mom!" Dyamonde chided. "Whatever happened to 'please'?"

Damaris laughed and passed the syrup to Mrs. Daniel, but not before she'd poured plenty on her second stack of banana pancakes.

"Yum!" said Damaris.

"You can say that again!" Dyamonde chimed in.

"Yum!"

Make Way for Dyamonde Daniel

"Clean, direct prose and strong, clear characterizations make this an appealing early chapter book, while Christie's stylized, dynamic drawings give it a fresh look. A welcome addition to the steadily growing list of beginning chapter books with African American protagonists, this is a promising start for the Dyamonde Daniel series." —*Booklist*

"Deals well with some complex issues, gently touching on the complexity without oversimplifying the feelings behind the situation."
—*The Bulletin of the Center for Children's Books*

"City youngsters will welcome a story set in their world—the world of small businesses, nosy old folks, small apartments and people from many cultures, and new readers will welcome the familiar situations, large font and ample white space. Gregory's familiar black-and-white sketches add a hip, urban feel to the tale. Here's hoping this series kick-off leads to many more stories about best friends Dyamonde and Free." —*Kirkus Reviews*

Rich: A Dyamonde Daniel Book

"Fast-paced, believable urban school situations . . . make this a particularly relevant series entry for chapter-book readers. Christie's light pen-and-ink sketches bring these good-hearted characters to life. Young readers will wish they had a friend like Dyamonde." —*Kirkus Reviews*

"Vividly drawn African American characters . . . looks at the sensitive issues of poverty and homelessness from different angles and in a reassuringly matter-of-fact way. Expressive ink drawings illustrate this fine beginning chapter book." —*Booklist*

"Nikki Grimes's beginning chapter book features inviting characters, an engaging story, and a look at the challenges of poverty. It also poses the question: What makes one truly rich? The rhythm, pacing, and tone of Grimes's narration is captivating." —*School Library Journal*

Almost Zero:
A Dyamonde Daniel Book

HORACE MANN UPSTANDERS BOOK AWARD

THE CHICAGO PUBLIC LIBRARY'S
BEST OF THE BEST READING LIST

"The family and friend dynamics are pitch perfect, and Grimes portrays third-grader Dyamonde with a very realistic balance of self-confidence and self-doubt as she adjusts to new ideas. . . . Honest yet funny."

—*The Horn Book*

"Christie's modern black-and-white illustrations are perfect for the urban setting. Dyamonde's readers will enjoy seeing a strong, smart African American girl face the same challenges they do. A treasure." —*Kirkus Reviews*

"An enjoyable story with a good life lesson. . . . The moral of the story is delivered in an endearing, accessible package. Grimes's style is easygoing and straightforward, her characters real and engaging. Christie's sketches in thick lines of black ink add to the book's appeal."

—*School Library Journal*

Born and raised in New York City, **Nikki Grimes** began composing verse at the age of six and has been writing ever since. She is the critically acclaimed author of numerous award-winning books for children and young adults, including Coretta Scott King Award winner *Bronx Masquerade*, Coretta Scott King Honor winner *The Road to Paris* and *New York Times* bestseller *Barack Obama: Son of Promise, Child of Hope* (illustrated by Bryan Collier). In addition to a Coretta Scott King Award and four Coretta Scott King Honors, her work has received accolades such as the NCTE Award for Excellence in Poetry for Children, *Booklist* Editors' Choice, ALA Notable, Bank Street College Book of the Year, *Horn Book* Fanfare, *American Bookseller* Pick of the List, Notable Social Studies Trade Book, NAACP Image Award Finalist, and the Golden Dolphin Award, an award given by the Southern California Children's Booksellers Association in recognition of an author's body of work. She lives in Corona, California.

Visit her at www.nikkigrimes.com.